Dear Parents,

ASPCA Rescue Readers series tells stories of animal adoptions from the animal's point of view! Written with warmth and gentle humor, these leveled texts are designed to support young readers in their growth while connecting to their passion for pets.

Level 2 in this series is designed for early readers who need short simple sentences, familiar vocabulary, informative illustrations, and easier spelling patterns to give them support as they practice to become fluent readers.

When you're reading with your children, you can help by encouraging them to think about using more than one strategy to unlock new words. Successful readers solve words in a variety of ways. Here are some tips you might share with your child:

- Take a picture walk before you read so you can preview the story.

- Sound out the word, remembering that some letters say more than one sound.

- For long words, cover up the end so you can figure out the beginning first.

- Check the picture to see if it gives you some clues.

- Skip over the word and read a little farther along. Then come back to it.

- Think about what is happening in this story. What would make sense here?

Learning to read is an exciting moment in a child's life. A wonderful way to share in that moment is to have conversations about the books after reading. Children love talking about their favorite part, or connecting the story to their own lives. I hope you'll enjoy sharing in the fun as your children get to know McKinley and all the other adopted pets that are part of this series. Happy reading!

M.S. Ed.

...list, Bank Street College of Education

6|17
AR Level

AR Points

Quiz #

Published by Studio Fun International, Inc.
44 South Broadway, White Plains, NY 10601 U.S.A. and
Studio Fun International Limited,
The Ice House, 124-126 Walcot Street, Bath UK BA1 5BG
Illustration © 2015 Studio Fun International, Inc.
Text © 2015 ASPCA®
All rights reserved.
Studio Fun Books is a trademark of Studio Fun International, Inc.,
a subsidiary of The Reader's Digest Association, Inc.
Printed in China.
Conforms to ASTM F963
10 9 8 7 6 5 4 3 2 1
SL1/09/14

***The American Society for the Prevention of Cruelty to Animals (ASPCA®) will
receive a minimum guarantee from Studio Fun International, Inc. of $25,000
for the sale of ASPCA® products through December 2017.
Comments? Questions? Call us at: 1-800-217-3346**

Library of Congress Cataloging-in-Publication Data

Froeb, Lori.
 I am McKinley / by Lori C. Froeb.
    pages cm -- (Rescue readers)
  Summary: "Inspired by a joyous real-life ASPCA animal rescue and
adoption story, read about the everyday details of family life through
the curious eyes and mind of a newly adopted pet. Meet McKinley. She's a
great dog and she's just been adopted! Come along with her as she meets her
new family and explores her new home"-- Provided by publisher.
  ISBN 978-0-7944-3310-9 (paperback)
1. Dogs--Juvenile fiction. [1. Dogs--Fiction. 2. Pet
adoption--Fiction.] I. Title.
  PZ10.3.F9335Iam 2015
  [E]--dc23
                    2014030658

I Am McKinley

written by
McKinley

(with help from Lori C. Froeb)

illustrated by Miki Sakamoto

studio BOOKS

White Plains, New York • Montréal, Québec • Bath, United Kingdom

Woof, woof!
My name is McKinley
and my life is great!

Can you see my tail wagging?

It's always wagging
because I belong to Tammy.
She is the most wonderful
person in the world!

5

Tammy is my girl.

She takes very good care of me!

Her hugs are the best.

Her treats are the best.

She knows the ones I like.

They taste like BACON!

Tammy might be small,

but her heart is big.

I love Tammy!

Do you know what else I love? Walks!
Where are we going today?
I really, really, really hope it's the park!

Tammy holds my leash.
I try not to tug,
but sometimes I can't help it.

Yup, it is the park!

The park is my favorite place to go.

What is that sound?

Who is that new dog?

What is that new smell?

I want to roll in it!

Tammy laughs when I roll in the grass.

She rubs my belly.

It feels so good!

Do you see the birds in the tree?

Shhh... I have to be very quiet.

I sneak up to the tree.

Woof! Woof! WOOF!

Look at them go!

It works every time!

I have dog friends, too.

Today Buffy and Pepper are here.

Pepper likes to play tag.

I do, too!

Run, Pepper, run!

Catch me, Pepper!

Tammy chases us.

Buffy just watches.

She doesn't like to get dirty.

15

Before I met Tammy,
my life was not very nice.
I was cold and lonely.
I had no home.

I saw dogs walking with
their people.
I wished I had a person, too.

I wagged my tail
every time someone
talked to me.

Every day I hoped to find my person.
One day, the wagging worked!

A nice lady took me to a shelter.
I rode in her car.
I didn't know where I was going,
but I couldn't wait to get there!

At the shelter
I got food to eat.
Wow! I was hungry!
I also got a bath.
I don't like baths.
But this one felt good.

When I was dry and fluffy,
everyone said, "What a cute dog!"
That's what Tammy McKinley said
the first time she saw me!

I yipped and wagged my tail.
Pick me! Pick me!
I was so happy
when Tammy took me home.
My tail never stopped wagging.

I was even happier when I got a name.

McKinley!

The McKinleys want everyone to know

I belong to them.

A lot has happened since that day.
My family was surprised
when I had four puppies.
Yup! I became a mom!

Tammy named the puppies
Max, Coco, Jack, and Gus.
She loves them as much as I do.

The puppies grew big and strong.

Tammy promised to find them good homes.

And she did.

I still see my puppies all the time.
They belong to Tammy's friends!

Do you want to meet my puppies?

They are coming to my house to play!

I tug on the leash

as we walk home from the park.

Sometimes I still can't help it!

I just can't wait to see

Coco, Jack, Max, and Gus!

My life is great!

I love my family.

I love my home.

And you know what?

I even love my baths.

The only thing better than today
is tomorrow.
I am lucky to be me!

Meet the real McKinley!

McKinley was one of many dogs being kept at a shelter in Murray, Kentucky when Tamara came looking for new companion. McKinley was pregnant, making her a tough dog to place in a home. But Tamara didn't mind. She saw McKinley and knew she was the perfect dog for her. McKinley had her puppies soon after being adopted and Tamara worked to find new homes for every one of them. Now McKinley is happy to be in her forever home with her beloved Tamara!

For more information on how to help animals, go to **www.aspca.org/parents.**